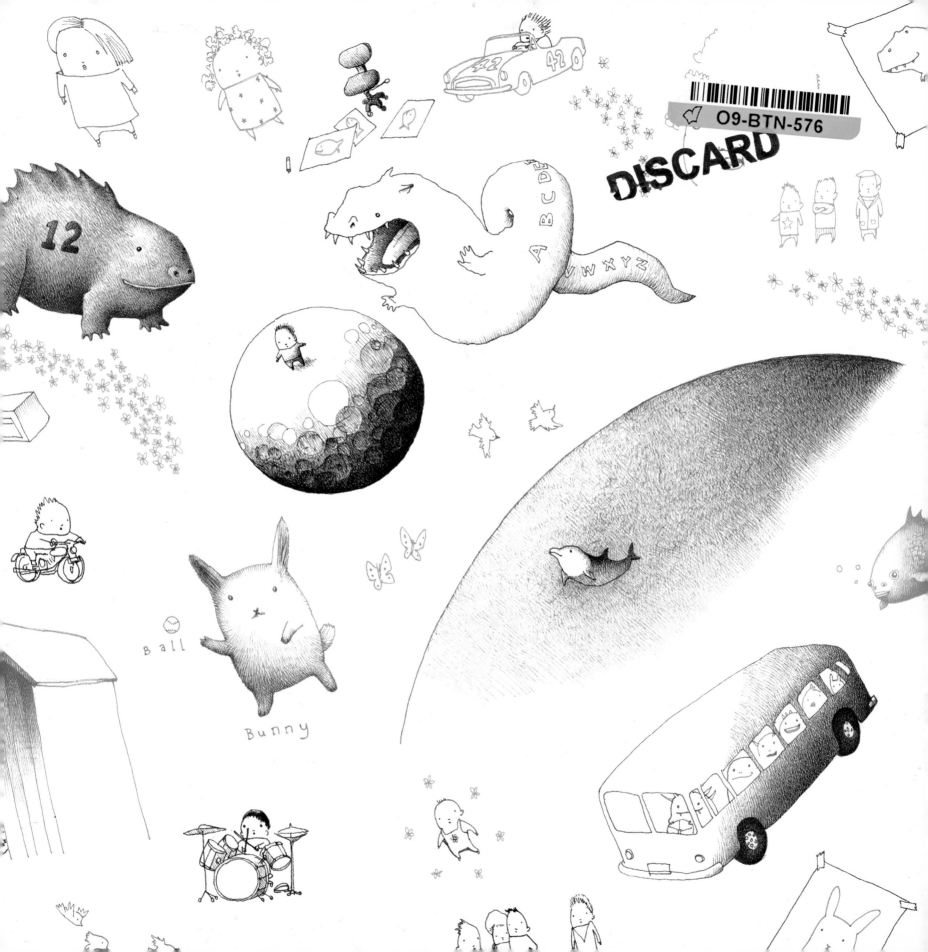

To Mary Ellen, Jeremy, and Margaret

Henry Holt and Company, LLC

Publishers since 1866

175 Fifth Avenue, New York, New York 10010

mackids.com

Henry Holt® is a registered trademark of Henry Holt and Company, LLC.

Copyright © 2012 by Peter McCarty

Library of Congress Cataloging-in-Publication Data

McCarty, Peter.

The monster returns / Peter McCarty. — 1st ed.

p.   cm.

Summary: When the monster that Jeremy created threatens to return, Jeremy enlists his neighbors
to help him with a creative solution to the problem.

ISBN 978-0-8050-9030-7 (hc)

[1. Monsters—Fiction. 2. Drawing—Fiction. 3. Friendship—Fiction.] I. Title.

PZ7.M478403Mo 2012   [E]—dc23   2011014349

First Edition—2012 / Designed by Patrick Collins

The artist used pen and ink and watercolors on watercolor paper to create the illustrations for this book.

Printed in China by South China Printing Company Ltd., Dongguan City, Guangdong Province

1 3 5 7 9 10 8 6 4 2

The Monster Returns

Peter McCarty

Henry Holt and Company

NEW YORK

One beautiful day,
Jeremy was up in his room.

Jeremy didn't like to be disturbed
when he was drawing.

But what was this?

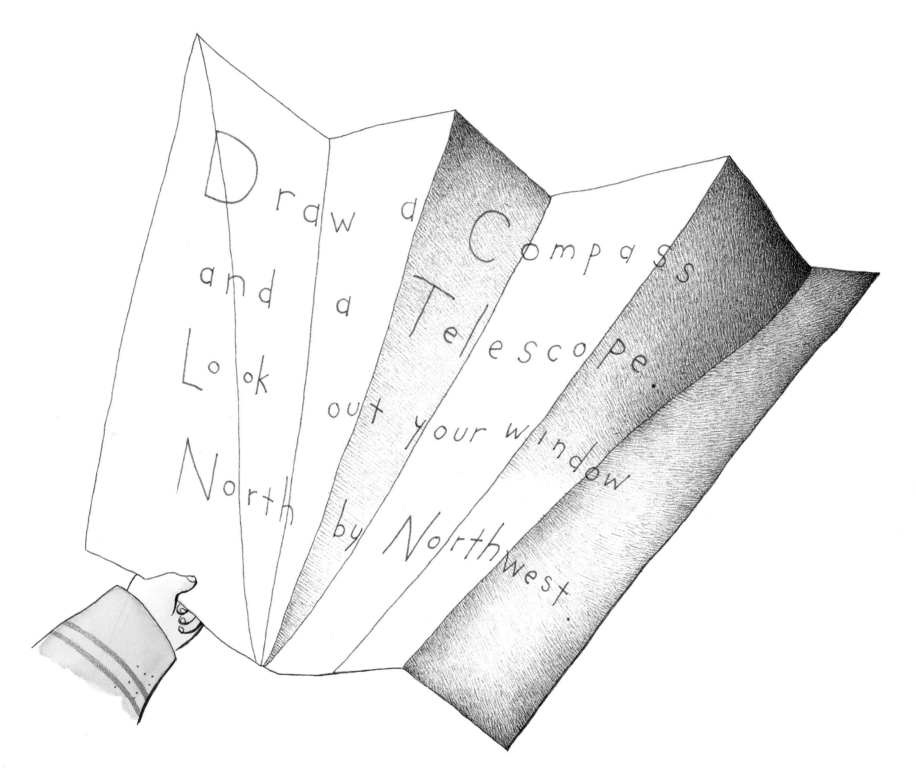

It was a note.

Jeremy did what the note said.

What did he see?

It was the monster again!
At that moment,
Jeremy's telephone rang.

"I'm bored," said the monster.
"And I'm coming back!"

Jeremy had to think fast.

He called down to the neighbors,
"Do you want to come up to my room?"

"Okay," they said.

Jeremy gave them
each a fancy pen
and told them what to do.

First, Millie drew a pink monster
with flowers.

Owen drew an orange one
with flippers.

Anthony's monster had blue spots
and a curly tail.

Sam's monster was short and purple.
Martha's was tall and brown.

Leon drew a big green monster
with sharp teeth and stripes.

"Great job, everybody," Jeremy said.
"Quiet now. Here he comes!"

Jeremy's monster had returned!

He walked up the stairs.

He banged on Jeremy's door.
When the door opened...

"SURP

RISE!"

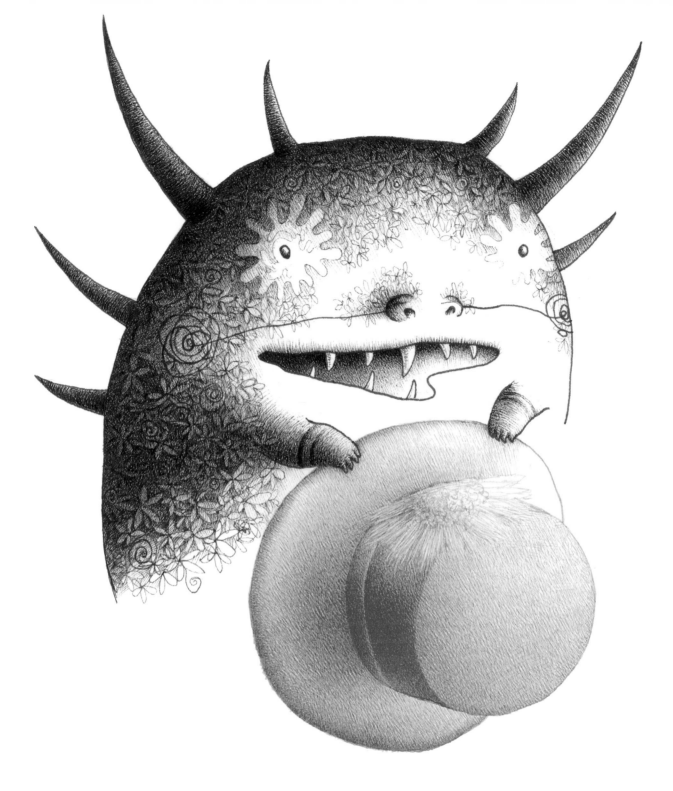

"Friends for me?" the monster said.

"Yes," Jeremy said.

"Friends for you *and* for me."

The Monster Returns

324.1

DOG BONE

43

26